[美]玛丽

MAGIC TREE HOUSE

神奇树屋

20

DINGOES AT DINNERTIME

解除魔咒

主译:蓝葆春　蓝纯

湖北长江出版集团
湖北少年儿童出版社

★ 名人推荐 ★

陈乃芳：美国麻省大学高级访问学者，曾任驻比利时使馆兼驻欧盟使团教育处参赞，北京外国语大学校长；第九、十届全国政协委员，政协外事委员会委员，中国高等教育学会高教管理研究会副理事长，中国教育国际交流协会常务理事，《国际论坛》杂志主编；由泰国王储授予名誉教育学博士、由英国兰卡斯特大学校长亚历山大公主授予名誉法学博士，并有多部论著。

亲爱的少年读者们：

你们好！最近我有机会阅读了一套英汉双语版的系列丛书，名字叫做《神奇树屋》(Magic Tree House)，作者是当今美国最著名的少儿读物作家之一——玛丽·波·奥斯本。几乎全美国的少年儿童都喜欢读她写的《神奇树屋》，把她当作自己的好朋友。我虽早已年过六旬，但是我和美国的小朋友们一样，一拿到这套书就爱不释手，不到两天就全部读完了。

你们也许要问：您为什么这么喜欢这套书呢？

我的回答是：首先，作者的创作思路紧紧扣住了小读者渴求知识、喜欢冒险、充满好奇和富于幻想的心理特点，成功地打造了神奇树屋这个平台。神奇树屋挂在森林里最高的一棵橡树的顶上，里面堆满了图书。它的神奇之处在于小读者翻开其中的任何一本书，指着书中的一幅插图许愿说"我希望到那里去"，梦想就能即刻实现。其次，作者充分发挥"魔法"的作用，轻松自如地引领读者穿越时空，周游世界。从见识白垩纪恐龙时的翼龙和冰河时代最凶猛的野兽剑齿虎，到体察今日的澳洲袋鼠；从了解美国早期荒凉西部的牛仔生活，到欣赏古代中国牛郎织女的传奇故事；从游览古埃及的金字塔到身陷2000多年前中国的秦始皇陵；从遭遇加勒比海的海盗到幸会东方的日本忍者；从历险维苏威火山的爆发到探秘亚马孙河的热带雨林……真是随心所欲，神游八方。再者，作者成功地塑造了杰克和安妮这一对小兄妹，通过他俩的所见、所闻、所思、所想和亲身历险，把历史故事、神话传说、科普知识、人文传统等栩栩如生地展现在读者面前，让你如同身临其境。最后，这套书不仅内容丰富有趣，而且文字浅显易懂，让人捧读之下，不忍释手。

为了把这套优秀的少儿读物介绍给全中国的中小学生，湖北少儿出版社特别邀请了我的老同学、老同事、老朋友蓝葆春爷爷和他的女儿——北京外国语大学的蓝纯教授负责全套丛书的汉语翻译。他们的译文既忠实于原文，又琅琅上口。所以我建议小读者们在阅读过程中先读译文，再读原文，这样一书两用，既增长了知识，又提高了英语，算是一举两得吧。

最后我想感谢两位译者请我作序，让我有了先睹为快的机会。也感谢湖北少儿出版社为全中国的中小学生们献上的这份大礼。

祝你们阅读愉快！

陈乃芳

目录

最后一件礼物

The Last Gift

安妮抓住绳梯开始往上爬。

杰克跟在她后面爬进了树屋。

一条小狗坐在夕阳射进来的光圈里，摇着尾巴。

安妮坐在门廊的台阶上，凝视着通往蛙溪湾的街道。

"嘿，杰克，"她说，"你听到了吗？"

杰克正坐在她旁边看书。

"听到什么？"他问。

"泰迪在叫我们呢！"安妮说。

"你在开玩笑吧。"杰克说。可他也向街道那头望去，听着动静。

远处隐隐约约传来狗的叫声。

汪！汪！

杰克开心地笑了。

"你听到了！"安妮说。

"是，"杰克回答，"你说得对，咱们该出发了。"

他站起身，抓起背包。

　　"我们很快就回来！"安妮冲着屏风的门喊了一声。

　　"别耽误吃晚饭！"爸爸喊道。

　　"不会的！"杰克说。

　　他和安妮跑到街上，跑进蛙溪湾树林。

　　很快他们就来到那棵最高的橡树前。

　　神奇树屋就在上面。一个小黑鼻子从树屋的窗户里探出来。

　　"嘿，小傻瓜！"安妮喊道，"我们来了！"

　　汪！小狗快乐地应了一声。

　　安妮抓住绳梯开始往上爬。

　　杰克跟在她后面爬进了树屋。

　　一条小狗坐在夕阳射进来的光圈里，摇着尾巴。

　　"你好，泰迪！"杰克说。

　　他们拥抱泰迪，小狗也舔着他们俩。

"莫根的字条还在这儿。"安妮说。

"是。"杰克回答。他现在都能背出字条上的留言了。

> 这条小狗中了魔咒,需要你们
> 的帮助。要救小狗,你们必需得到
> 四件特殊的礼物:
> 　一件来自大海沉船,
> 　一件来自蓝色草原,
> 　一件来自遥远的森林,
> 　还有一件来自袋鼠。
> 　一定要聪明、勇敢、小心。
>
> 　　　　　　　　　　莫根

字条旁边是他们前三次旅行得到的礼物。

1. 一块来自泰坦尼克号的怀表

2. 一根来自草原雄鹰的羽毛

3. 一朵来自印度大森林的荷花

"我们只需要从袋鼠那儿得到一份礼物了，"安妮说，"然后泰迪就可以从咒语中解脱出来。"

"我们得去一趟澳大利亚，"杰克说，"那儿是袋鼠生活的地方。"

"酷！"安妮说。

泰迪呜呜地叫了一声，前爪挠着角落里的一本书。

杰克把书捡了起来。

"我跟你说什么来着？"他说。

他把封面给安妮看。书的名字是《澳大利亚历险记》。

"好极了！"安妮说。她看着泰迪，"准备好去见袋鼠了吗？"

汪！汪！

杰克翻开书，找到有各种动物插画和一幅大的森林插画的那一页。他指着森林。

"我希望我们能去那儿。"他说。

风开始猛刮。

树屋开始旋转。

它越转越快。

然后一切归于静止。

完全的静止了。

2 贪睡的家伙

Sleepyhead

"啊，真可爱！"安妮小声说。

那家伙正在酣睡。它长着两只又圆又大的耳朵，一个黑鼻子，毛茸茸的身体，脚上还长着长而弯曲的爪子。

杰克睁开眼睛。炙热、耀眼的阳光洒进树屋。

"好漂亮的帽子！"安妮说。

她和杰克都戴着帽子。

"我想这样可以防晒吧。"杰克说。

他和安妮向窗外望去，泰迪也向外望。

树屋降落的地方是一片灌木丛林。丛林里的植物被太阳晒得发蔫，树木都呈干褐色。

"嗬，这地方需要雨水。"杰克说。

他屈腿坐在地上，在那本《澳大利亚历险记》的插画里查看他们着陆的地方。

他读道：

澳大利亚的森林经常遭遇干旱。干旱就是长时间不下一滴雨。但在其他季节里同样一片森林又会因暴雨袭击而遭受水灾。

杰克拿出笔记本写道：

干旱=无雨

"嘿，杰克，"安妮说，"你没闻到野炊的香味儿吗？"

杰克闻了闻，真的有一股炊烟的味道。

杰克向窗外望去，看见一缕轻烟在远处的树林上方飘动。

"可能有人在那边露营吧。"杰克说。

"咱们过去看看。"安妮提议。

杰克将笔记本和那本澳大利亚书放进背包。

"把泰迪也放进去吧。"安妮说。

杰克把小狗也塞进背包，
跟着安妮下了绳梯。

双脚刚落地，一阵热风就
差点把他们的帽子吹跑了。

"露营者肯定是在那边。"安妮说。

她指了指蓝天下飘浮的炊烟,他们开始穿越一片晒干的开阔地。

沿途不断看到灌木丛和干枯的树木。蜥蜴在干裂的地面上爬来爬去。

汪!汪!泰迪在背包里叫了起来。

"哇!"杰克惊叹道。

一对样子很滑稽的大鸟从一簇灌木后面走了出来。

它们比杰克还要高,身体肥胖,腿和脖子又瘦又长。

"你们是谁呀?"安妮问这对奇异的鸟。

杰克打开背包,拿出那本澳大利亚书。他找到了一幅鸟的画。"它们是鸸鹋。"他说。他大声地读道:

鸸鹋是一种体型大而不会飞的鸟,跑得很快,时速可达30英里。

"哇,那可真够快的!"安妮说。

汪!泰迪从杰克的背包里跳了出来,对着那两只怪鸟乱叫。

鸸鹋傲慢地瞥了小狗一眼,转身骄傲地走开了。

杰克在笔记本上写道:

鸸鹋

骄傲的鸟

不会飞

"快看,一只活的玩具熊!"安妮说。

杰克闻声抬头。

安妮向空地边的一棵树跑了过去。一只"活的玩具熊"正偎依在树杈上。

"啊,真可爱!"安妮小声说。

那家伙正在酣睡。它长着两只又圆又大的耳朵,一个黑鼻子,毛茸茸的身体,脚上还长着长而弯曲的爪子。

"这是考拉熊。"杰克说。

"嗨，贪睡的家伙。"安妮对考拉熊说。

她轻拍着它柔软的皮毛。考拉熊睁开大眼睛，安静地看着安妮。

杰克在澳大利亚书上找到了考拉熊的画儿，他读道：

考拉熊其实并不是熊，而是像袋鼠一样的一种有袋动物。

有袋动物的妈妈总是把幼崽装在腹部的育儿袋里。

"真神奇！"安妮说。

杰克继续读道：

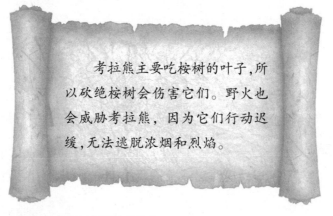

考拉熊主要吃桉树的叶子，所以砍绝桉树会伤害它们。野火也会威胁考拉熊，因为它们行动迟缓，无法逃脱浓烟和烈焰。

杰克又掏出笔记本写道：

野火对考拉熊是一种威胁

"怎么啦，瞌睡虫？"安妮问考拉熊，"你感觉还好吧？"

"别担心，"杰克说，"听听这一段——"

他继续读书上的介绍:

考拉熊像袋鼠一样,喜欢晚上活动,白天睡觉,因为白天阳光太强。'考拉'这个名字的意思是'不喝',因为考拉熊很少喝水。它们从吃的树叶中获取水分。

杰克舔了舔嘴唇，觉得有些渴了。

"说到水，我也感到渴了。"他说。

"我也是。"安妮应和道。

泰迪在一旁喘气，好像它也渴了。

"咱们去找那些宿营者吧，"杰克叹了口气，"没准他们能给我们一点水喝。"

杰克把泰迪放进背包，把书夹在腋下，以备随时查找。

他们继续往前走。突然传来一阵巨大、尖厉的咯咯声。

"呀！"安妮惊讶道。

"什么东西？"杰克问。

大脚

Big Foot

　　袋鼠和安妮开始相互转着圈地跳,好像在跳舞似的。

　　杰克不敢相信袋鼠能跳得如此优美,似乎是腾空飞翔,接着又轻轻落地,像蝴蝶一样轻盈。

刺耳的叫声又从干燥的空气中传了过来。

泰迪也叫了起来。

杰克和安妮在开阔地里四处张望，可是很难辨别声音来自何方。

可怕的咯咯声又响起来了。

"在那儿！"安妮说。

她指着桉树上的一只鸟，那鸟的羽毛是褐色的，大脑袋，长嘴。

它盯着树下的杰克和安妮，又咯咯地叫了一声。

"奇怪！"杰克说。

他在书上找到了那只鸟：

> 笑翠鸟是澳大利亚最著名的一种鸟。关于它还有一首流行歌曲。笑翠鸟又叫"笑驴"，因为它发出的奇怪的叫声很像驴。

"我知道那首歌！"安妮说。她开始唱了起来。

"笑翠鸟坐在老桉树上,快乐的灌木王子就是他……"

杰克在笔记本上写道：

笑翠鸟————一个大怪物

安妮停了下来。"快看,"她说,"那边还有一个奇怪的家伙。"

"在哪儿？"杰克问。

安妮指了指一个浅浅的土坑,一个蓝褐色的家伙正躺在那里。

"是活的吗？"杰克问。

他们朝那家伙走了几步。

"看样子在呼吸。"安妮说。

原来那是个仰躺着的动物,双爪交叉放在胸前。

它长着一双大脚,两只大耳朵,脸型很像鹿,还有一条很

长的尾巴，和一个肥肥大大的肚子。

就在这时，一个小脑袋从它的肚子里探了出来。

"哇！"杰克吃惊地叫起来。

"啊！原来是一只袋鼠和它的宝宝！"安妮说。

"太好了！"杰克说。"记得吗？我们需要从袋鼠那儿得到一份礼物呢！"

他们的声音把袋鼠妈妈吵醒了。它从浅坑里跳了起来。

它愤怒地盯着杰克和安妮。袋鼠宝宝在育儿袋里偷偷往外看。

袋鼠妈妈生气地跺了一下脚。

"啊,很抱歉!"安妮说,"我们不是有意吵醒你的。"

袋鼠妈妈好奇地瞟了安妮一眼,然后向她跳了一大步。

安妮学着她的样子,也向袋鼠跳了一步。

袋鼠又跳了一步。

安妮也跳了一步。

袋鼠和安妮开始相互转着圈地跳,好像在跳舞似的。

杰克不敢相信袋鼠能跳得如此优美,似乎是腾空飞翔,接着又轻轻落地,像蝴蝶一样轻盈。

他在书中找到了袋鼠的介绍:

> 袋鼠是最有名的有袋动物。母袋鼠把幼崽放在育儿袋里随身携带。科学家称袋鼠为"大豆荚",意思是"大脚"。一双大脚使袋鼠比世界上任何其他动物都跳得高。一只大袋鼠在奔跑中的一跃能跳过一辆校巴。

"别再搞蹦跳比赛了,安妮,"杰克喊
道,"它能领先你一英里呢。"

他掏出笔记本写道:

> 袋鼠
> "大脚"
> 可以跳过一辆校巴!

袋鼠妈妈又开始跺脚了。

"怎么啦?"安妮问。

袋鼠呆立在那里。

汪汪汪!泰迪在杰克的背包里咆哮。

近处的灌木丛里传出响动。

过了一会儿,三条狗悄悄地爬进了开阔地。它们毛色沙
黄,相貌狰狞。

泰迪又乱叫起来。

可那些狗还是蹑手蹑脚地向袋鼠爬去。

突然，袋鼠妈妈腾空一跃避开了那几条狗。

狗在后面紧追不舍。

"站住！"安妮喊道，"站住！不许追袋鼠！"

袋鼠在跳跃时，在半空中转了个弯，所以落地时朝着不同的方向。它就这样在岩石和灌木丛中跳来跳去。

那几条野狗一面嗥叫一面追赶袋鼠妈妈和袋鼠宝宝。

袋鼠宝宝

Joey

　　杰克蹲下身来，抚摸小袋鼠棕色的皮毛。真的很柔软，是杰克所触摸过的最柔软的皮毛了。

　　那个害羞的小家伙瞪着一双褐色的大眼睛盯着杰克，仍在颤抖。

"啊,不行!"安妮叫喊着,"我们得去救它!"

她拔腿去追那几条狗。

汪!汪!汪!泰迪在杰克的肩头上叫。

杰克把书夹在腋下,去追安妮。他在干燥发裂的地面上奔跑,经过枯萎的灌木丛和七零八落的桉树。

杰克的眼睛紧盯着跑在他前面的安妮。他看到她突然停了下来,转过身,双膝跪下。

"出什么事了?"他高喊。

"快过来看!"安妮说。

杰克跑到安妮身旁。只见袋鼠宝宝就在她身边的草地上,浑身发抖。

"别害怕。"安妮说。她看着杰克,"袋鼠妈妈呢?为什么丢下小宝宝?"

"我也不知道。"杰克说。

他把背包放到地上,打开《澳大利亚历险记》。泰迪跟着跳了出来。

它想嗅一嗅袋鼠宝宝。

"别吓着他,泰迪。"安妮说。

泰迪退后坐下，彬彬有礼地打量袋鼠宝宝。

杰克翻开《澳大利亚历险记》，找到一幅袋鼠宝宝的画儿。他读道：

> 袋鼠最大的敌人是澳洲野狗。当袋鼠妈妈被澳洲野狗追赶时，它可能将幼崽从育儿袋里扔出来，因为没有育儿袋中的额外负担，它能跳得更快更远。这样它就能把澳洲野狗从它的宝宝身边引开。在摆脱了野狗之后，袋鼠妈妈会回到幼崽身边。

"啊，杰克，"安妮伤心地说，"我真希望它妈妈能逃脱野狗的追赶。"

"我也一样。"杰克说。

"喂，小家伙，"安妮轻轻地拍着袋鼠宝宝，"它软绵绵的，杰克。"

杰克蹲下身来，抚摸小袋鼠棕色的皮毛。真的很柔软，

是杰克所触摸过的最柔软的皮毛了。

那个害羞的小家伙瞪着一双褐色的大眼睛盯着杰克，仍在颤抖。

"别害怕，小家伙，"安妮说，"你妈妈很快就会回来找你的。"

小袋鼠跳着离开了杰克和安妮。它向杰克立在地上的背包蹦去。

它纵身一跃就头朝下钻进了背包！只见它整个身子都进到了背包里面，可是一双大脚却露在外头。然后转过身来偷偷地看杰克和安妮。

他们俩都笑了起来。

"它把你的背包当成育儿袋了！"安妮说，"我知道怎么办了。把背包反过来挂在胸前，这样它就会觉得像妈妈背着它一样。"

杰克把澳大利亚书放到地上，安妮帮他把背包挂在胸前，而不是背在背上。小袋鼠还挺沉！

"瞧！"安妮说，"你看上去就像袋鼠妈妈。"

"噢，真不轻啊！"杰克说。

可他还是轻轻地拍打着小家伙柔软的皮毛。

　　"别担心,"他对小袋鼠说,"你可以一直待在这儿等你妈妈回来。"

　　"喂,小家伙,想吃点草吗?"安妮问。

　　她从地上扯起一把草送到小袋鼠面前。

　　小袋鼠起劲地吃着,眼睛一直盯着安妮。

　　"真希望它妈妈很快就会回来找它。"她担心地说。

　　"是呀!"杰克说。

　　他抬眼在干枯的森林里四处搜寻。没有袋鼠妈妈的踪影。

　　但是杰克看到了别的什么东西。

　　"快看!"他对安妮说。

　　天空中那一缕轻烟已变成了一大块黑云。杰克注意到树木燃烧的味道变浓了。

　　"那些露营者在干什么呢?"安妮说,"是在生营火吗,还是在干别的什么?"

　　杰克突然感到一阵恐惧。

　　"要是……"他说,"要是……"

　　远处,一棵树突然着火了。

　　"这是野火!"他说。

5 野火！

Wildfire!

　　杰克和安妮一个抱着小袋鼠，一个抱着考拉熊，跟着泰迪的吠声在烟火弥漫的森林里穿行。

　　终于，他们来到一块巨石旁。

解除魔咒

*Dingoes
at
Dinnertime*

"野火？"安妮问。

"这些树木都这么干燥，所有的东西都会烧起来的！"杰克说，"我们得离开这儿。"

"我们不能丢下小袋鼠！"安妮说。

"把它带上！"杰克说。

"可是如果他妈妈回来找它，发现它不见了怎么办呀？"安妮问。

"我们没有选择了。"杰克说。

就在这时，笑翠鸟怪叫着从空中飞过。

鸸鹋也以最快的速度奔跑。

空气变得越来越呛人。大火迅速蔓延。

"快！"杰克说，"我们得赶在树屋烧毁前赶回去！"

"树屋在哪个方向？"安妮问。

"我也拿不准。"杰克说。

浓烟把树顶都遮住了。杰克的眼睛被烟熏得生疼。

"管不了那么多了，"他说，"我们得逃出浓烟。快！"

杰克和泰迪转身就跑。袋鼠宝宝把脑袋藏在杰克的背包里。

"我会赶上你们的！"安妮说，"我得取点东西！"

"什么？"杰克叫喊着。

可是安妮已经朝另一个方向冲了出去。

"回来！"杰克高喊，"安妮！"

断裂的树枝不断掉落，到处浓烟翻腾。

汪！汪！

"安妮！"杰克呼喊着。

他被烟呛着了。他一面咳嗽一面揉眼睛，空气越来越滚烫。

他别无选择，只有跑走。

汪！汪！泰迪在前边叫。

"快一点，安妮！"杰克无望地喊着，转身去追泰迪。

他在灌木丛中跌跌撞撞，只能跟着泰迪的叫声摸索前进。他感到背包越来越沉，只好用双手托着继续往前跑。

突然他听到安妮在叫他。

杰克停了下来。

"这儿！这儿！这儿！我们在这儿！"他高声喊道，"快，跟着我们！"

安妮在热烫的烟雾中出现了。她咳

嗷着，眼泪不住地往下流。

她抱着那只考拉熊！

"快呀！"杰克喊道，"跟着泰迪！"

汪！汪！

杰克和安妮一个抱着小袋鼠，一个抱着考拉熊，跟着泰迪的吠声在烟火弥漫的森林里穿行。

终于，他们来到一块巨石旁。

汪！汪！

泰迪站在一处石脊上。它身后是一个洞穴的入口。

透过烟雾，杰克几乎看不见泰迪。

泰迪又叫了一声，消失在洞穴里。

"跟着它！"安妮说。

手拉手
Hand to Hand

汪！汪！

"看来我们只能跟着泰迪的叫声走了，"安妮说，"咱们手拉着手吧。"

她把空着的手伸向杰克。杰克握紧安妮的手，又伸出另一只手去摸洞穴的墙壁。小袋鼠在他的背包里不安分地动。

杰克和安妮爬上石脊，踏进洞穴。洞里的空气比洞外干净多了，凉爽多了。

"我什么都看不见！"杰克说。

他摸了摸袋鼠宝宝的脑袋。

"我也是。"安妮说。

汪！汪！

"看来我们只能跟着泰迪的叫声走了，"安妮说，"咱们手拉着手吧。"

她把空着的手伸向杰克。杰克握紧安妮的手，又伸出另一只手去摸洞穴的墙壁。小袋鼠在他的背包里不安分地动。

杰克和安妮走进黑暗中。

汪！

泰迪不停地叫，领着他们往前走。

汪！

汪！

汪！

汪！

突然，杰克感到有个什么东西重重地打了一下他的腿。

他停住脚步,倒吸了一口气。

"怎么了?"安妮问。

汪!

原来是泰迪!它摇着尾巴打杰克的腿。

"怎么回事,伙计?"杰克问。

泰迪发出了一声嚎叫。

就在它嚎叫的时候,一件令人惊奇的事情发生了。

一条白线开始在空中发光,而且越变越粗,直到看起来像一条巨蛇。在蛇的身体下面出现了几只发光的手印。

杰克感到安妮握紧着他的手。

"好像是画在墙上的。"安妮说。

"但是画的是什么呢?"杰克轻声地问。

"不知道。"安妮说。

她放开杰克的手,把自己的手放进画中的一个手印里。

杰克也把手放进一只手印里。

尽管壁画发出红光,但石壁是光滑而冰凉的,好像还在呼吸。

一个幽灵般的口哨声从黑暗中传来,接着是一声巨大的

隆隆声。

"什么声音？"杰克迅速把手从墙上拿开。

隆隆声再次传来。

"听起来像打雷！"安妮说。

汪！汪！

"泰迪准备离开了！"安妮说。

她抓住杰克的手，他们转身退回原路，继续跟着泰迪的叫声往前走。

汪！

他们跟着小狗走呀走，终于看到一束白光。

"闪电，"安妮说，"打雷了！闪电了！我们到了洞穴的尽头了！耶！"

安妮拉着杰克跑向洞口，冲了出去，冲进倾盆大雨中。

7 雨, 雨, 雨

Rain, Rain, Rain

　　大雨变成了细雨,细雨又变
成了飘洒的雨丝。
　　他们继续等……
　　杰克越来越伤心。

雨点落在杰克的头上，也落在小袋鼠的脑袋上。雨水淋着安妮，也淋着泰迪和考拉熊。

安妮张开嘴喝雨水。

杰克也一样。雨水的味道比他喝过的任何水都好。

杰克回头看森林，薄薄的雾气正在烧焦的地面和燃烧着的灌木丛中蒸腾。

大雨在扑灭野火。

"你现在安全了，"安妮对考拉熊说，"我会把你放回一棵桉树的树杈上，让你完成你的小睡。"

"我看见一棵没有烧着的树了！"杰克说。

他们走到那棵未烧毁的桉树旁。安妮把考拉熊放在树杈上。

"接着睡吧，"她轻柔地说，"就把这场野火当成一个梦。"

"晚安。"杰克说。

考拉熊似乎对他们展颜一笑，接着它就闭起双眼继续睡觉，好像一点都没被打扰似的。

杰克叹了口气，向四周看了看。

"嗬,"他说,"我们真幸运,来了一场暴雨。"

安妮也笑了。

"这不仅是幸运,"她说,"这是魔法。"

"魔法?"杰克说。

"是呀……那发光的手印和蛇,"安妮说,"不知怎么的,它们就带来了暴雨。"

"可这没有道理呀!"杰克说。

小袋鼠在他的背包里骚动起来。杰克突然想起件事儿。

"哎呀,我们得把小袋鼠送回它妈妈丢下它的地方,"他说,"要不然它妈妈就找不到它了。"

"那地方在哪儿呢?"安妮问。

"我也不知道。"杰克说。

他环视一下雨中灰暗的森林。一切看起来都是原样。

"泰迪能找到那地方!"安妮说。

小狗连叫都没有叫一声,就动身穿越潮湿、泥泞的地面。

杰克和安妮跟在它后面。因为背着小袋鼠,杰克的背开始感到疼。

汪!汪!

　　杰克和安妮赶上了泰迪。它正站在那本澳大利亚书旁！书淋湿了，但是没有烧坏。

　　"好啊，我们找到了！"安妮说。

　　"不错！"杰克说，"我是把书落在我们发现小袋鼠的地方的！"

　　"泰迪又帮了我们一个大忙！"安妮说。

　　她轻轻地拍了拍小狗的脑袋。

　　"谢谢，泰迪！"杰克说。

　　他捡起澳大利亚书。书皮打湿了，可书页看起来还好。杰克把书夹在腋下，小袋鼠从背包里偷偷往外看。

　　"别担心，小家伙，"安妮说，"我们就待在这儿，等你妈妈回来找你。"

　　如果它已经来过了……杰克有点担心。

　　杰克和安妮站在雨里，和泰迪、小袋鼠一起等待。

　　他们等呀，等呀。

大雨变成了细雨,细雨又变成了飘洒的雨丝。

他们继续等……

杰克越来越伤心。

也许袋鼠妈妈已经来过了,又走了;也许它被澳洲野狗抓住了;也许它被野火烧死了。

杰克不敢看安妮,不敢说话。

"我知道你在想什么。"安妮终于开口了。

杰克轻轻地拍着小袋鼠的头,叹了口气。

"咱们再等一会儿吧,"他说,"如果它妈妈还不回来,我们就把它带回家——"

汪!泰迪轻轻地叫了一声。

"听!"安妮说。

杰克竖起耳朵听。

那声音开始很模糊,但是越来越响。

那是一种湿软的声音,一种踏步的声音,是大脚快步拍击泥巴的声音。

8 彩虹蟒

The Rainbow Serpent

　　土著艺术家们将彩虹蟒绘制在洞壁或树皮上。举行特殊仪式时，他们会把手印画在这条神奇的蟒蛇身上，以示对彩虹蟒的尊敬。

袋鼠妈妈从树林里跳了出来。

它在离杰克、安妮、泰迪和小袋鼠十英尺远的地方停住脚步。

一时间大家都静止不动,好像屏住呼吸似的。

小袋鼠想跳出杰克的背包。

"等一等。"杰克说。

他把背包放到地上。

小袋鼠一跃而出。

它跳了一下……再跳一下……然后一头栽进妈妈的育儿袋里。

小袋鼠在育儿袋里转了个身,偷偷地看着杰克和安妮。

"耶!"杰克和安妮一起高兴地说。他们笑着拍手,如释重负。

"回到妈妈身边,小袋鼠很高兴呢!"安妮说。

"它妈妈也很高兴。"杰克说。

袋鼠妈妈仔细地打量自己的小宝宝,用爪子拍着小家伙的脑袋。

然后它用温和的眼神看着杰克和安妮。

"它在向我们道谢呢！"安妮说。

"不用谢！"杰克说。

"别放在心上，"安妮说，"你的小宝宝很棒！"

袋鼠微微点点头，屈身用前爪从潮湿的草丛里捡起一小块树皮。

袋鼠把树皮交给杰克和安妮。

杰克接过树皮。

"噢，好极了，"他轻轻地说，"这就是我们从袋鼠那儿得到的礼物。"

袋鼠一下子蹦到空中，在烧焦的森林里优雅地跳走了。

"谢谢！"杰克喊道。

"再见！"安妮喊道，"祝你好运！"

汪！汪！泰迪叫了几声。

雨已经停了。杰克仔细观察那片树皮。树皮上有细小的花纹，就

像洞穴壁上那幅蛇的绘画。

"我想我知道蛇的意思了！"杰克说。

他翻开那本封皮淋湿了的澳大利亚书，小心翻动潮湿的书页，找到了一幅蛇的图画。

"听着，"杰克说，他读道：

> 最早的澳大利亚人被称为"土著居民"。他们已在澳洲居住了40,000年。他们的神话故事发生在一个被称为"梦幻时代"的年代。在梦幻时代里有一条彩虹蟒，它能送来救命雨。

土著艺术家们将彩虹蟒绘制在洞壁或树皮上。举行特殊仪式时，他们会把手印画在这条神奇的蟒蛇身上，以示对彩虹蟒的尊敬。

"明白了吗？"安妮说，"一切都解释得清清楚楚！"

"解释什么？"杰克问。

"我们把手放在彩虹蟒的画儿上，"她说，"那就像是一种特殊仪式，所以彩虹蟒就送来了雨将野火扑灭。"

汪！泰迪又叫了。

杰克皱起眉头。

"可彩虹蟒不是一个真的动物呀，"他说，"它生活在梦幻时代，不是现在。"

安妮笑了。

"那你怎么解释那个呢？"她指着天空说。

雨云已散，太阳又出来了。

一条彩虹凌空出现在澳大利亚的蓝天上。

"啊，嘀！"杰克轻声地说。虽然气温已经升上来了，可他还是颤抖不已。

"是泰迪把我们领到壁画边的，"安妮说，"我们得谢谢它。"

"它怎么知道洞穴里的彩虹蟒呢？"

杰克问。

"我不是告诉过你吗,"安妮说,"它有魔法。"

他们低头看着那条小狗。泰迪歪着脑袋,似乎在笑。

"嘿,我们现在已经有四件礼物了!"安妮说。

"啊,对!"杰克说。

"咱们回家吧,看看泰迪的咒语是不是已经解除了!"安妮说。

汪!汪!

杰克把《澳大利亚历险记》和树皮放进背包,然后他们朝着树屋的方向,穿越潮湿的、充满雾气的森林。

"我希望树屋没有被烧毁!"他说。

他们走过开阔地,桉树林和灌木丛。

树屋正在等他们呢。

"它还在那儿!"安妮说。

她抓住绳梯往上爬。

杰克把泰迪放进背包也跟着上来了。

进了树屋，泰迪从背包里爬了出来，用前爪去抓那本宾夕法尼亚书。

汪！汪！

"行了，行了！"杰克说。他指着一幅蛙溪湾的画儿说："我希望我们能到那儿去！"

"飞越彩虹！"安妮说。

风又开始刮。

树屋开始旋转。

它越转越快。

然后一切归于静止。

完全静止了。

9 哪个男孩?

What Boy?

这时一件奇妙的事情发生了。
转瞬之间……
在旋风般的急转中……
泰迪变了。

"欢迎归来。"一个温柔甜美的声音传来。

杰克睁开双眼。

原来是莫根！他们有好久没见到莫根了。

"莫根！"安妮喊道。

她伸开双臂抱住那位魔法师。杰克也跳起来拥抱莫根。

"见到你们俩很高兴。"莫根说。

汪！汪！

"见到你也很高兴。"莫根笑着跟小狗打招呼说。

"瞧，"安妮说，她从杰克的背包里掏出那块绘有花纹的树皮，"一件来自袋鼠的礼物。"

"我们现在已经得到全部的四件礼物了！"杰克说。

"干得不错。"莫根说。

她拿起第一件礼物，那是泰坦尼克号的怀表。

"从前有一个浪费时光的男孩，"莫根说，"这块表教育他时间是非常珍贵的，必须聪明地利用。"

莫根又拿起第二件礼物，那是从勒科塔印第安人那儿得到的鹰的羽毛。

"有时那男孩不敢独立面对困难，这根鹰的羽毛教育他一个小生命也可以长成最勇敢的人。"

莫根又拿起印度大森林的荷花。

"那男孩有时不尊重大自然，"她说，"这朵荷花告诉他大自然拥有许多奇观。"

莫根最后拿起那块绘有彩虹蟒的树皮。

"有时那男孩不想学习关于历史和其他地方的知识，这幅画告诉他，在古代人的传统中有很多神奇、奥妙和智慧。"

"哪个男孩？"杰克问。

"你在说谁呀？"安妮也问。

莫根并没有马上回答。她把手放在杰克和安妮的肩膀上。

"谢谢你们帮助那个男孩学到这些东西，"她说，"谢谢你们帮助他解脱了咒语。"

"哪个男孩？"杰克又问。

汪！汪！汪——！

杰克和安妮望着泰迪。

这时一件奇妙的事情发生了。

转瞬之间……

在旋风般的急转中……

泰迪变了。

他不再是一条狗。

他是个小男孩。

梦幻时代

Dreamtime

　　"我们跟泰迪一起经历的冒险真是太棒了——噢,我是说泰德,你说呢?"

　　"是呀,"杰克说,"就像……"他在寻找一个确切的词,"就像……"

　　"就像生活在梦幻时代!"安妮说。

那男孩跪在地上。

"来见见我的来自卡默洛特的小助手吧。"莫根说。

男孩抬起头。他长着一张友善的、有点小雀斑的脸和一双忽闪忽闪的黑眼睛,头发跟泰迪的皮毛一个颜色。他看上去比杰克要大一点,大约十岁的样子。

"我恢复人形了吗?"他问。

"是的,你恢复人形了。"莫根说。

男孩跳了起来,一把将她搂住。

"谢谢您!"他叫道。

"我希望你下次使用我的魔法书里的咒语前一定先问问我。"莫根说。

男孩羞怯地一笑。

"我保证!"然后他看着杰克和安妮,"我不小心将自己变成了一条狗。"他说。

安妮大笑起来。

"不过作为狗我至少经历了许多次令人兴奋的探险!"他说。

"你曾是一条了不起的狗呢!"安妮说,"我们都喜欢泰

迪。你真正的名字是什么？"

"要是你们喜欢，尽管叫我泰迪好了，"男孩说，"要不叫泰德也行。"

"好吧，泰德！"安妮说。

杰克只是点头。他仍然处在震惊之中。

"泰德正在接受培训，准备去我的卡默洛特图书馆工作，"莫根说，"他在魔法方面有难得的天赋。"

"酷！"安妮说。

"你——你给了我们太多帮助。"杰克终于说话了。

"啊，不，是你们俩帮助了我，"泰德说，"你们帮我解脱了咒语，而我找到了可以带回家的新故事。"

"是吗？"安妮问。

泰德点点头。

"泰坦尼克号故事、白衣野牛女子的故事、受伤老虎的故事，还有彩虹蟒的故事。"他说。"我一回家就把它们写下来，这样人们就可以在莫根图书馆里读到这些故事了。"

"我想我们该出发回家了。"莫根说。

"噢，"安妮伤心地说，"这么快吗？"

"是呀！"杰克也说。他也很伤心。

"我知道我们还会再见面的。"泰德说。

"希望如此。"杰克说。

"我也一样，"安妮说，"再见！"

她爬下绳梯。

杰克拽着背包，带着一颗沉重的心跟在后面。

到达地面时，他们抬头仰望。

莫根和泰德站在窗前，在夕阳的照射下他们俩似乎都闪闪发光。

"神奇树屋会很快回来找你们的，"莫根说，"我保证。"

她挥了挥手,他们也挥挥手。

"再见,杰克!再见,安妮!"莫根说。

"汪!"泰德说。

转瞬之间……

在旋风般的急速转动中……

神奇树屋不见了。

杰克和安妮注视着那棵孤零零的树久久不转神。

"回家吃晚饭?"安妮轻轻地问。

杰克点点头。

他们一语不发地穿过蛙溪湾树林,杰克感到有点头晕。

他们回到熟悉的街道,太阳已经落山。一群黑色的鸟儿从晚霞染红的天空飞过。

　　两人一路往家走，安妮首先打破了沉默。

　　"我们跟泰迪一起经历的冒险真是太棒了——噢，我是说泰德，你说呢？"

　　"是呀，"杰克说，"就像……"他在寻找一个确切的词，"就像……"

　　"就像生活在梦幻时代！"安妮说。

　　"对！"杰克说。他笑了。

　　是的，的确如此。

解除魔咒

● 在澳洲生活的动物中,有 170 个不同类型的有袋动物,包括考拉熊、袋熊、袋鼠和沙袋鼠(很像袋鼠,但是比袋鼠小)。卷尾袋鼠是唯一生活在澳洲以外的有袋动物。

● 袋鼠在澳洲已经生存了两千五百万年。澳大亚大约有一千九百万人口,袋鼠的数量是这个数字的 10 倍！一只袋鼠跳跃的时速约为 11 英里,爆发时可达 30 英里。

● 考拉熊以橡胶树汁为生。橡胶树又叫桉树。桉树油可以治疗感冒和流感。桉树散发的强烈气味为很多人喜欢。

● 澳大利亚土著居民曾把澳洲野狗当猎犬使用。

● 澳洲是世界上最小、最平坦的一块陆地。澳大利亚是世界上唯一独占一整块陆地的国家。这块陆地大约 3 百万平方英里,相当于美国除去阿拉斯加和夏威夷之后的面积。

● 有一个时期,地球上的各大洲曾是一个巨大的陆地块。大约 20 亿年以前,澳洲从这块陆地中分裂开来。因为澳洲与其他陆地隔离,所以澳洲动物与其他各洲动物的进化进程不一样。

解除魔咒

DINGOES AT DINNERTIME

解除魔咒

DINGOES AT DINNERTIME

CONTENTS

1

The Last Gift

Annie sat on the porch steps. She stared down the street at the Frog Creek woods.

"Hey, Jack," she said. "Do you hear it?"

Jack sat next to her. He was reading a book.

"Hear what?" he said.

"Teddy's calling us," said Annie.

"You're kidding," said Jack. But he looked down the street and listened, too.

A faint bark came from the distance.

Arf! Arf!

A big smile crossed Jack's face.

"You hear it!" Annie said.

"Yep," said Jack. "You're right. Time to go."

He stood up and grabbed his backpack.

"Be back soon!" Annie shouted through the screen door.

"Don't be late for dinner!" their dad called.

"We won't!" said Jack.

He and Annie ran down the street and into the Frog Creek woods.

Soon they came to the tallest oak.

There was the magic tree house. A little black nose stuck out the window.

"Hi, silly!" Annie called. "We're coming!"

Arf! Came a happy bark.

Annie grabbed the rope ladder and started climbing.

Jack followed her up into the tree house.

A small dog sat in a circle of afternoon sunshine. His tail wagged.

"Hey, Teddy!" said Jack.

Jack and Annie hugged Teddy. And the dog licked both of them.

解除魔咒

Dingoes
at
Dinnertime

"Morgan's note is still here," said Annie.

"Yep," said Jack. He knew the note by heart now.

> *This little dog is under a spell*
> *and needs your help. To free him, you*
> *must be given four special things:*
> A gift from a ship lost at sea,
> A gift from the prairie blue,
> A gift from a forest far away,
> A gift from a kangaroo.
> *Be wise. Be brave. Be careful.*
> *Morgan*

Beside the note were the gifts from their first three trips:

1. a pocket watch from the Titanic

2. an eagle's feather from the prairie skies

3. a lotus flower from a forest in India

"We just need to get a gift from a kangaroo," said Annie, "and Teddy will be free from his spell."

"We must be going to Australia," said Jack. "That's where kangaroos live."

"Cool," said Annie.

Teddy whined and scratched at a book lying in the corner.

Jack picked it up.

"What'd I tell you?" he said.

He showed the cover to Annie. The title was *Adventure in Australia.*

"Great," said Annie. She looked at Teddy. "Ready to meet a kangaroo?"

Arf! Arf!

Jack opened the book. He found a page with small pictures of different animals and a big picture of a forest. Jack

pointed at the forest.

"I wish we could go there," he said.

The wind started to blow.

The tree house started to spin.

It spun faster and faster.

Then everything was still.

Absolutely still.

2

Sleepyhead

Jack opened his eyes. Glaring hot sunlight flooded into the tree house.

"Neat hats," said Annie.

She and Jack were both wearing hats.

"I think they will protect us from the sun," said Jack.

He and Annie looked out the window. Teddy looked out, too.

The tree house had landed in a scrubby forest filled with droopy plants and dry brown trees.

"Man, this place needs rain," said Jack.

He sat back on his heels and looked at the picture of where they had landed in the Australia book.

He read：

Australia's forests go through times of drought （say DROWT）. A drought is a long period of time without any rain. The same forest can be flooded by heavy rains at other times of the year.

Jack pulled out his notebook and wrote：

drought = no rain

"Hey, Jack," said Annie. "Doesn't it smell like a cookout?"

Jack sniffed the air. It *did* smell like a cookout.

Jack looked out the window. A wisp of smoke floated above some trees in the distance.

"Maybe people are camping over there," Jack said.

"Let's go see," said Annie.

Jack put his notebook and the Australia book into his backpack.

"Put Teddy in there, too," said Annie.

Jack slipped the little dog into the pack. Then he followed Annie down the ladder.

When they stepped onto the ground, the hot wind nearly blew their hats off.

"The campers must be over there," said Annie.

She pointed at the smoke in the blue sky. They started

walking across a sun-baked clearing.

They passed bushed and scrawny trees. Lizards ran over the dry, cracked ground.

Arf! Arf! Teddy barked from Jack's pack.

"Whoa!" said Jack.

A pair of huge, funny-looking birds walked out from behind a bush.

They were taller than Jack. They had fat bodies, long, skinny legs, and long, skinny necks.

"Who are *you?*"Annie asked the strange pair.

Jack opened his pack and took out the Australia book. He found a picture of the birds.

"They're emus," he said. He read aloud:

The emu(say EE-myoo) is a large bird that doesn't fly. It can run as fast as thirty miles per hour.

"Wow, that's fast," said Annie.

Arf! Teddy jumped out of Jack's backpack and barked at the strange birds.

The emus gave the little dog a haughty look. Then they turned and walked proudly away.

Jack wrote in his notebook:

Emus

proud birds

don't fly

"Look, a *live* teddy bear!" said Annie.

Jack looked up.

Annie ran to a tree at the edge of the clearing. The "live teddy bear" was nestled in the fork of the tree.

"Aww, it's so cute!" whispered Annie.

The creature was fast asleep. He had large round ears, a black nose, and a furry body. His feet had long, curved claws.

"It's a koala bear," said Jack.

"Hi, sleepyhead," Annie said to the koala.

She patted his soft fur. He opened his big eyes and looked calmly at her.

Jack found a koala picture in the Australia book. He read:

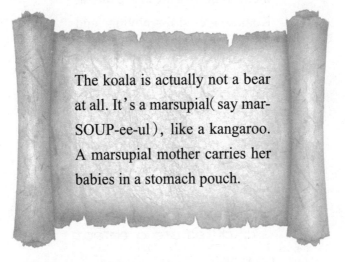

The koala is actually not a bear at all. It's a marsupial(say mar-SOUP-ee-ul), like a kangaroo. A marsupial mother carries her babies in a stomach pouch.

"That's neat," said Annie.

Jack kept reading:

Koalas mostly eat the leaves of gum trees, so cutting down gum trees to clear land has hurt them. Wildfires are also a threat. Koalas are slow-moving and can't escape the smoke and flames.

Jack pulled out his notebook and wrote：

wildfires are a threat to koalas

"What's wrong, sleepyhead?" Annie asked the koala.

"Don't you feel well?"

"Don't worry," said Jack. "Listen to this—"

He read more from the book:

> Koalas, like kangaroos, are active at night and sleep during the day, when the sun is hot. The name "koala" means "no drink," because koalas rarely drink water. They get moisture from the leaves they eat.

Jack licked his lips. His mouth felt dry.

"Speaking of water," he said, "I'm thirsty."

"Me, too," said Annie.

Teddy was panting, as if he was thirsty, also.

"Let's find those campers," said Jack, sighing. "Maybe they can give us some water."

Jack put Teddy back into his pack. He tucked the book under his arm, in case he needed to look something up.

They began walking again. Suddenly, there was a loud, harsh cackle.

"Yikes," said Annie.

"What was *that?*" said Jack.

Big Foot

The loud cry rang again through the dry air.

Teddy barked.

Jack and Annie turned around in the clearing. It was hard to tell where the sound was coming from.

The terrible cackle came again.

"There!" said Annie.

She pointed at a bird in a gum tree. The bird had brown feathers and a large head with a long beak.

It stared down at Jack and Annie. Then it let out another cackle.

"Weird," said Jack.

He found the bird in his book and read：

> The kookaburra（say KOOK-uh-burr-uh）is thc best-known bird of Australia. These is even a popular song about it. The kookaburra is also called the "laughing donkey."
>
> This is because the strange sound it makes reminds people of a braying donkey.

"I know that song!" said Annie. She began singing：

"*Kookaburra sits on the old gum tree-ee. Merry, merry king of the bush is he-ee...*"

Jack wrote in his notebook：

kookaburra—
a big kook

Annie stopped singing. "Hey," she said. "There's another weird thing."

"Where?" said Jack.

Annie pointed to a big bluish tan lump lying in a shallow, dusty hole.

"Is it alive?" said Jack.

They stepped closer to the big lump.

"It looks like it's breathing," said Annie.

The lump was an animal lying on its back. Its paws were crossed over its chest.

It had huge feet, large ears, a face like a deer's, and

a very long tail. It also had a *very* fat stomach.

Just then, a small head peered out of its stomach.

"Whoa!" said Jack.

"Oh, wow! It's a kangaroo with her baby in her pouch!" said Annie.

"Great!" said Jack. "Remember, we have to get a gift from a kangaroo!"

Their voices woke the kangaroo. The animal jumped up from her shallow bed.

She glared at Jack and Annie. Her baby peeked out of her pouch.

The mother kangaroo gave an angry stamp.

"Oh, we're sorry!" Annie said. "We didn't mean to wake you up. "

The kanagaroo eyed Annie curiously. Then she took a giant hop toward her.

Copying the kangaroo，Annie hopped toward the big animal.

The kangaroo hopped again.

Annie hopped.

The kangaroo and Annie began hopping around each other. They looked as if they were dancing.

Jack couldn't believe how graceful the kangaroo was. She seemed to fly through the air，then land as softly as a butterfly.

He looked up"kangaroo" in his book and read：

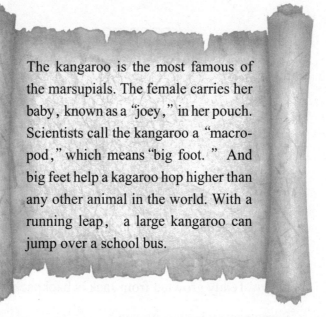

The kangaroo is the most famous of the marsupials. The female carries her baby, known as a "joey," in her pouch. Scientists call the kangaroo a "macro-pod," which means "big foot." And big feet help a kagaroo hop higher than any other animal in the world. With a running leap, a large kangaroo can jump over a school bus.

"Forget the hopping contest，Annie，" Jack called. "She can out-hop you by a mile. "

He pulled out his notebook and wrote：

kangaroo

"big foot"

Can jump over a

school bus!

The kangaroo began stamping her feet again.

"What's wrong?" said Annie.

The kangaroo froze.

Grrrr! Teddy growled from Jack's backpack.

Some nearby bushes moved.

A moment later, three dogs crept silently into the clearing. They were sand-colored and mean-looking.

Teddy growled once more.

But the dogs crept toward the kangaroo.

Suddenly，the mother kangaroo sprang into the air，
away from the dogs.

The dogs chased after her.

"Stop!" cried Annie. "Stop! Leave her alone!"

As the kangaroo jumped， she turned in midair and
landed facing a different direction. She then zigzagged over
rocks and bushes.

Howling，the wild dogs raced after the kangaroo
and her baby.

4

Joey

"Oh, no!" cried Annie. "We have to save her!"

She took off after the dogs.

Arf! Arf! Arf! Teddy barked over Jack's shoulder.

Jack ran after Annie with the book under his arm. He ran over the dry, cracked ground, past scrubby bushes and scattered gum trees.

Jack kept his eye on Annie, running ahead of him. He saw her stop suddenly. She turned and dropped to her knees.

"What happened?" he shouted.

"Come look!" she said.

Jack reached Annie. Beside her in the grass was the baby kangaroo. It was trembling.

"Don't be scared," Annie was saying. Then she looked at Jack. "Where's his mom? Why did she drop him?"

"I don't know," said Jack.

He put his pack on the ground and opened the Australia

book. Teddy jumped out of the pack.

The little dog tried to sniff the baby kangaroo.

"Don't scare him, Teddy," Annie said.

Teddy sat back and watched politely.

Jack opened the Australia book and found a picture of

a baby kangaroo. He read:

> The biggest enemy of the kangaroo is the dingo, the wild dog of Australia. When a mother kangaroo is chased by dingoes, she may throw her joey out of her pouch. Without the extra weight in her pouch, she can leap faster and farther. She then leads the dingoes away from her baby. If she escapes the dingoes, she returns to the joey.

"Oh, Jack," Annie said sadly. "I hope his mother escapes from the dingoes."

"Me, too," said Jack.

"Hi, Joey," said Annie. She gently patted the baby kangaroo. "He's so soft, Jack."

Jack knelt down and touched the brown fur. It *was* soft, the softest fur he had ever felt.

The shy little kangaroo stared at Jack with big brown eyes and trembled.

"Don't be scared, Joey," Annie said. "Your mom's going to come back for you."

Joey jumped away from Jack and Annie. He hopped toward Jack's pack, which was sitting on the ground.

The baby kangaroo took a giant leap and dived headfirst into the pack! His whole body went inside, but his big feet stuck out. Then he turned himself over and peeked out

at Jack and Annie.

They both laughed.

"He thinks your pack is a pouch!"said Annie. "I know. Put it on backward. It will feel like when his mom carries him. "

Jack put his Australia book on the ground. Then Annie helped him put the pack on his chest instead of on his back. The joey was heavy!

"There," Annie said."You look *just* like a mother kangaroo. "

"Oh, brother. " said Jack.

But he patted the baby's soft fur.

"Don't worry," he said to Joey. "You can stay in there till your mom gets back. "

"Here, Joey, would you like some grass to eat?" ask-

ed Annie.

Annie scooped up a handful of grass and gave it to the kangaroo.

He munched the grass, keeping his big eyes on Annie.

"I hope his mom comes back for him soon," she said worriedly.

"Yeah," said Jack.

He looked around the dry forest. There was no sign of the mother kangaroo.

But Jack saw something else.

"Look," he said to Annie.

The wisp of smoke in the sky had turned into a big black cloud. Jack noticed the smell of burning wood was much stronger.

"What are those campers doing?" said Annie. "Are

they making a bonfire now or what?"

A feeling of dread came over Jack.

"What if ..." he said. "What if ..."

In the distance，a tree suddenly burst into flames.

"We're looking at a wildfire!" he said.

Wildfire!

"Wildfire?" said Annie.

"The woods are so dry, everything's starting to burn!" said Jack. "We have to get out of here. "

"We can't leave Joey," said Annie.

"We'll take him with us!" said Jack.

"But what if his mom comes back for him and he's not here?" said Annie.

"We don't have a choice," said Jack.

Just then, the kookaburra flew through the sky, cackling.

The emus raced by at top speed.

The air was getting smokier and smokier. The fire was spreading quickly!

"Come on!" said Jack. "We have to get back to the tree house before it burns down!"

"Which way's the tree house?" said Annie.

"I'm not sure," said Jack.

Smoke hid the treetops. Jack's eyes stung.

"Forget it," he said. "Let's just get away from this smoke. Come on!"

Jack and Teddy turned to go. The baby kangaroo hid his head inside Jack's pack.

"I'll catch up!" said Annie. "I have to get something!"

"*What?*" cried Jack.

But Annie had dashed off in the other direction.

"Come back!" Jack shouted. "Annie!"

Branches cracked and fell from the trees. Smoke billowed everywhere.

Arf! Arf!

"Annie!" Jack cried.

Jack choked on the smoke. He coughed and rubbed his eyes. The air was getting hotter.

He had no choice. He had to run.

Arf! Arf! Teddy barked from somewhere ahead.

"Hurry, Annie!" Jack called helplessly. Then he took off after Teddy.

He stumbled blindly through the brush. All he could do was follow the sound of Teddy's barking. His pack felt heavier and heavier. He held it up with his arms and kept going.

Suddenly, Jack heard Annie calling him.

Jack stopped.

"Here! Here! Here! We're here!" he shouted. "Come on! Follow us!"

Annie appeared through the haze of the hot smoke. She was coughing. Tears streamed from her eyes.

She was carrying the koala!

"Come on!" Jack cried. "Follow Teddy!"

Arf! Arf!

Jack and Annie carried Joey and the koala. They followed
Teddy's barking through the smoky, fire-filled forest.

Finally, they came to a giant rock.

Arf! Arf!

Teddy was standing on a ledge. Behind him was the
mouth of a cave.

Through the smoke, Jack could barely see the little dog.

Teddy barked again, then vanished inside the cave.

"Follow him!" said Annie.

6

Hand to Hand

Jack and Annie climbed onto the rock ledge and stepped into the cave. The air inside was cleaner and cooler than the air outside.

"I can't see anything," said Jack.

He patted the head of the baby kangaroo.

"Me neither," said Annie.

Arf! Arf!

"I guess we'll have to follow Teddy's bark," said Annie. "Let's hold hands."

She held out her free hand to Jack. Jack took it. Then he put his other hand out and touched the wall. The joey moved in his pack.

Jack and Annie walked into the darkness.

Arf!

Teddy kept barking, leading them on.

Arf!

Arf!

Arf!

Arf!

Suddenly, Jack felt something thump against his leg. He stopped and gasped.

"What is it?" said Annie.

Arf!

It was Teddy! His tail was wagging and hitting Jack's leg.

"What is it, boy?" Jack asked him.

Teddy let out a howl.

As he howled, an amazing thing happened.

A white line began to glow in the air. The glowing line grew until it looked like a giant snake. Then glowing handprints appeared below the snake.

Jack felt Annie squeeze his hand.

"I think it's painted on the wall," she said.

"But what is it?" whispered Jack.

"I don't know," said Annie.

She let go of Jack and put her hand inside one of the painted handprints.

Jack did the same.

Despite the glowing painting, the rock felt smooth and cool. It almost seemed to breathe.

A ghost-like whistling sound came through the darkness. Then a loud boom!

"What's *that*?" Jack quickly took his hand off the wall.

The boom came again.

"It sounded like thunder," said Annie.

Arf! Arf!

"Teddy's leaving!" said Annie.

She grabbed Jack's hand. They turned back the way they had come and followed Teddy's barking again.

Arf!

They followed the little dog until they saw a flash of light.

"Lightning，" said Annie. "Lightning and thunder! We're at the front of the cave! Yay!"

Annie pulled Jack toward the mouth of the cave and out，into a pouring rain.

Rain, Rain, Rain

Rain fell on Jack's head and on Joey's head. Rain fell on Annie's head and on Teddy's head and on the koala's head.

Annie opened her mouth and drank the rainwater.

Jack did the same. The water tasted better than any water he'd ever drunk.

When Jack looked back at the woods，misty steam was rising from the charred ground and burning bushes.

The heavy rain was putting out the wildfire.

"You'll be safe now," Annie said to the koala. "I'll put you back in a nice gum tree. Then you can finish your nap."

"I see a tree that's not burned," said Jack.

They walked over to the unburned gum tree. Annie placed the koala in the fork of two branches.

"Go back to sleep now," she said softly. "Pretend the fire was all a dream."

"Good night," said Jack.

The koala seemed to smile at them. Then he closed his eyes and went to sleep, as if he'd never been disturbed at all.

Jack sighed and looked around.

"Man," he said, "we were lucky that a storm came."

Annie smiled.

"It wasn't just luck," she said. "It was magic."

"Magic?" said Jack.

"Yeah ... the glowing hands and the snake," said Annie. "Somehow they brought the storm."

"That doesn't make sense," said Jack.

Joey stirred in his pack. Suddenly, Jack remembered something.

"Hey, we have to get Joey back to the place where his mom left him," he said. "Or she won't be able to find him."

"Where was that place?" said Annie.

"I don't know," said Jack.

He looked around at the rainy gray forest. Everything looked the same.

"Teddy can find the spot!" said Annie.

Without even a bark, the little dog took off across the wet, muddy ground.

Once again, Jack and Annie followed him. Jack's

back was beginning to hurt from carrying Joey.

Arf! Arf!

Jack and Annie caught up with Teddy. He stood over the Australia book! It was wet, but not burned.

"Hurray, we found it!" said Annie.

"That's right!" said Jack. "I left our book in the spot where we found Joey!"

"Once again, Teddy helped us out," said Annie.

She patted the little dog's head.

"Thanks Teddy," Jack said.

He picked up the Australia book. The cover was wet, but the pages looked okay. The little kangaroo peeked out of his pack as Jack tucked the book under his arm.

"Don't worry, Joey," Annie said. "We'll stay right here till your mom comes back for you."

If she hasn't already come ... Jack thought worriedly.

Jack and Annie stood in the rain with Teddy and Joey and waited.

They waited and waited.

The rain turned to a drizzle. Then the drizzle turned to a light sprinkle.

Still, they waited ...

Jack grew sadder and sadder.

Maybe the mother kangaroo *had* come and left. Or maybe she had been caught by the dingoes. Or maybe she had been killed by the wildfire.

Jack was afraid to look at Annie, afraid to say anything.

"I know what you're thinking," she said finally.

Jack patted Joey's head and sighed.

"Let's wait a little longer," he said. "If she doesn't come back soon, we'll take him home with—"

Arf! Teddy barked softly.

"*Listen,*" said Annie.

Jack listened.

The sound was very faint at first. But then it grew louder.

It was a squishy sound. It was a squashy sound. It was

the sound of big feet slapping through mud!

The Rainbow Serpent

The mother kangaroo bounded out of the trees.

She landed ten feet away from Jack, Annie, Teddy, and Joey.

They all were still for a moment, as if they all were holding their breath.

Then Joey tried to jump out of Jack's backpack.

"Hold on," said Jack.

He put his pack on the ground.

The little kangaroo leaped out.

He leaped again ... then again ... and dived headfirst into his mother's pouch!

Joey turned himself over inside the pouch. Then he peeked out at Jack and Annie.

"Yay!" said Jack and Annie together. They laughed and clapped with relief.

"He looks happy to be home," said Annie.

"His mother looks happy, too," said Jack.

The mother kangaroo was gazing down at her joey. She patted his head with her small paws.

Then she looked at Jack and Annie with soft eyes.

"She's saying thank you to us," Annie said.

"You're welcome," Jack said.

"It was no problem," Annie told the kangaroo. "You have a great joey."

The kangaroo gave a little nod. Then she bent over and used a front paw to pick up a small piece of bark from the wet grass.

The kangaroo held the piece of bark out to Jack and Annie.

Jack took it from her.

"Oh, man," he whispered. "It's our *gift from a kangaroo.*"

The kangaroo then sprang into the air. She bounded gracefully away through the charred forest.

"Thanks!" called Jack.

"Bye!" called Annie. "Good luck!"

Arf! Arf! Teddy barked.

The rain stopped as Jack studied the piece of bark. There was a tiny painting on it. It was just like the snake painting in the cave.

"I wonder what the snake means," said Jack.

Jack opened the wet cover of the Australia book. He carefully turned the damp pages. He found a picture of the snake

painting.

"Listen," said Jack. He read:

> The first people of Australia are called "Aborigines"(say ab-uh-RI-J-uh-neez). They have lived there for 40, 000 years.Their myths take place in a time they call "Dreamtime." In Dreamtime, there is a Rainbow Serpent, who sends lifegiving rain.
>
> Aborigine artists paint the Rainbow Serpent on cave walls or on pieces of bark. In special ceremonies, they sometimes honor the Rainbow Serpent by painting their handprints on the magic snake.

"See?"said Annie."That explains everything!"

"Explains what?" said Jack.

"We put our hands on the painting of the Rainbow

Serpent，" she said. "It was like a special ceremony. So the Rainbow Serpent sent the rain to put out the wildfire. "

Arf! Teddy barked.

Jack frowned.

"But it's not a real creature，" he said. "It's in *Dream time*. Not *real* time. "

Annie smiled.

"Then how do you explain *that?*" she said. She pointed at the sky.

The rain clouds were gone. The sun had come back out.

A rainbow curved across the blue Australian sky.

"Oh，man，" whispered Jack. Though the air was warm again，he shivered.

"Teddy led us to the painting，" said Annie."We should thank him. "

"How did he know about the Rainbow Serpent in the

cave?" Jack asked.

"I told you," said Annie. "He has a touch of magic. "

They looked down at the little dog. Teddy titled his head and seemed to smile.

"Hey, we have all four gifts now!" said Annie.

"Oh, yeah!" said Jack.

"Let's go home and see if Teddy's spell is broken!" said Annie.

Arf! Arf!

Jack put the bark painting and the Australia book in his pack. Then they all headed through the wet, steamy forest in the direction of the tree house.

"I hope the tree house didn't get burned!" he said.

They went past the clearing, past the gum trees and bushes.

The tree house was waiting for them.

"It's still here!" said Annie.

She grabbed the rope ladder and started up.

Jack put Teddy in his pack and followed.

Inside the tree house，Teddy wiggled out of the pack.
He pawed the Pennsylvania book.

Arf! Arf!

"Okay，okay，" said Jack. He pointed at a picture of
the Frog Creek woods. "I wish we could go there!"

"Over the rainbow!" said Annie.

And the wind started to blow.

The tree house started to spin.

It spun faster and faster.

Then everything was still.

Absolutely still.

9

What Boy?

"Welcome back," came a soft, lovely voice.

Jack opened his eyes.

It was Morgan! They hadn't seen Morgan in a long time.

"Morgan!" cried Annie.

She threw her arms around the enchantress. Jack jumped up and hugged Morgan, too.

"It's good to see you both," said Morgan.

Arf! Arf!

"And it's good to see *you*, too," Morgan said, smiling at the little dog.

"Look," said Annie. She reached into Jack's pack and pulled out the piece of painted bark. "A gift from a kangaroo."

"We have all four gifts now," said Jack.

"Good work," said Morgan.

She picked up their first gift. It was the pocket watch from the *Titanic*.

"Once upon a time, there was a boy who wasted time," Morgan said. "This watch teaches him that time is very precious. It must be used wisely. "

Morgan picked up their second gift, the eagle's feather from the Lakota Indians.

"Sometimes the boy was afraid to stand up for himself, "she said."The eagle's feather teaches him that a small creature can be one of the bravest."

Morgan picked up the lotus flower from the forest in India.

"Sometimes the boy did not respect nature," she said. "This flower teaches him that nature holds many wonders. "

Morgan picked up the piece of bark with the painting of the Rainbow Serpent.

"Sometimes the boy didn't want to study other times and places. " she said. "This painting teaches him there is mystery, magic, and wisdom in the traditions of ancient peoples. "

"What boy?" Jack asked.

"Who are you talking about?" asked Annie.

Morgan didn't answer right away.   She placed her hands on Jack's and Annie's shoulders.

"Thank you, " she said, "for helping this boy learn his lessons. Thank you for breaking the spell. "

"What boy?" Jack asked again.

Arf! Arf! Arrrrrrf!

Jack and Annie looked over at Teddy.

Then something magical happened.

In a flutter of time...

in the spin of a whirlwind ...

Teddy was changed.

He was no longer a dog.

He was a boy.

10
Dreamtime

The boy was on the ground on his hands and knees.

"Meet my young helper from Camelot," said Morgan.

The boy glanced up. He had a friendly freckled face and twinkly dark eyes. His hair was the same color that Teddy's fur had been. He looked a bit older than Jack, about ten or so.

"Am I back?" he asked.

"You're back," said Morgan.

The boy leaped up and hugged her.

"Thank you!" he cried.

"And I hope next time you'll *ask* before trying the spells in my spell book," said Morgan.

The boy grinned sheepishly.

"I promise." Then he looked at Jack and Annie. "I accidentally changed myself into a dog," he said.

Annie laughed.

"But at least I got to have exciting adventures as a dog!" he said.

"You were a *great* dog," said Annie. "We liked you as

解除魔咒

Dingoes
at
Dinnertime

Teddy. What's your real name?"

"If you like, you can keep calling me Teddy," the boy said. "Or how about Ted?"

"Okay, Ted," said Annie.

Jack just nodded. He was still in shock.

"Ted is training to work in my library at Camelot," said Morgan. "He has a rare gift for magic."

"Cool," said Annie.

"You—you helped us a lot, Ted," said Jack, finally finding his voice.

"Oh, no, it was both of *you* who helped me," said Ted. "You helped break the spell. And I found new stories to take home."

"You did?" said Annie.

Ted nodded.

"The story of the *Titanic*, the story of White Buffalo Woman, the story of the wounded tiger, and the story of the Rainbow Serpent," he said. "I'll write them down as soon as I get home. So people can read them in Morgan's library."

"And home is where we must go now, I'm afraid," said Morgan.

"Oh," said Annie sadly. "That's too bad."

"Yeah," said Jack. He was sad, too.

"I know we will meet again someday," said Ted.

"I hope so," said Jack.

"Me, too," said Annie. "Bye!"

She started down the ladder.

Jack pulled on his pack. With a heavy heart, he followed.

When they got to the ground, they looked up.

Morgan and Ted were at the window. They both seemed to glow in the late afternoon light.

"The magic tree house will return for you soon," said Morgan. "I promise."

She waved, and they waved back.

"Good-bye, Jack and Annie," she said.

"Arf!" said Ted.

In a flutter of time...

in the spin of a whirlwind...

the magic tree house was gone.

For a long moment, Jack and Annie stared at the empty tree.

"Ready for dinner?" Annie asked softly.

Jack nodded.

He felt dazed as they walked silently through the Frog Creek woods.

When they came to their street, the sun was setting. A flock of black birds flew through the silvery pink sky.

Annie broke their silence as they headed for their house.

"We had great adventures with Teddy—I mean Ted— didn't we?" she said.

"Yeah," said Jack. "It was like ..." He searched for the right words. "Like ..."

"Like living in Dreamtime," said Annie.

"Yeah," said Jack. He smiled.

That was *exactly* what it was like.

图书在版编目（ＣＩＰ）数据

解除魔咒：英、汉/(美)奥斯本著；蓝葆春，蓝纯译. —武汉：湖北少年儿童出版社，2010.3

（神奇树屋：典藏版）

书名原文：Dingoes at Dinnertime

ISBN 978－7－5353－5003－9

Ⅰ.解… Ⅱ.①奥…②蓝…③蓝… Ⅲ.儿童文学—短篇小说—美国—现代—英、汉 Ⅳ.Ⅰ712.84

中国版本图书馆 CIP 数据核字(2010)第 040530 号

This translation published by arrangement with Random House Children's Books, a division of Random House, Inc.

Book #20-**Dingoes at Dinnertime** Text copyright ⓒ 1992 by Mary Pope Osborne

Magic Tree House™ is a trademark of Mary Pope Osborne, used under license.

著作权合同登记号：图字：17-2006-050

神奇树屋典藏版 20——解除魔咒

原　　著：[美]玛丽·波·奥斯本

责任编辑：叶　珺　梁　崴

整体设计：一壹图文

出　品　人：李　兵

出版发行：湖北少年儿童出版社

经　　销：新华书店湖北发行所

印　　刷：湖北恒泰印务有限公司

规　　格：880×1230　1/32　5.25 印张

印　　次：2010 年 4 月第 1 版　**2016年8月第10次印刷**

书　　号：ISBN 978－7－5353－5003－9

定　　价：14.00 元

业务电话：(027)87679179　87679199

http://www.hbcp.com.cn